black is brown is tan

Arnold Adoff

pictures by
Emily Arnold McCully

HarperCollins Publishers

Amistad

for

leigh   and   jaime

black   and   t a n

kiss   big   sister

       hug

       big   m a n

Amistad is an imprint of HarperCollins Publishers.

black is brown is tan
Text copyright © 1973 by Arnold Adoff Text copyright renewed 2001 by Arnold Adoff
Illustrations copyright © 2002 by Emily Arnold McCully Manufactured in China. All rights reserved.
For information address HarperCollins Children's Books,
a division of HarperCollins Publishers, 10 East 53rd Street, New York, NY 10022.
www.harperchildrens.com

Library of Congress Cataloging-in-Publication Data
Adoff, Arnold.
    Black is brown is tan / by Arnold Adoff ; pictures by Emily Arnold McCully.
    p.   cm.
    Summary: Describes in poetic form a family with a brown-skinned mother, light-skinned father, two children, and
their various relatives.
    ISBN 0-06-028776-4 — ISBN 0-06-028777-2 (lib. bdg.) — ISBN 0-06-443644-6 (pbk.)
    [1. Human skin color—Fiction.   2. Racially mixed people—Fiction.   3. Family life—Fiction.   4. Stories in
rhyme.]   I. McCully, Emily Arnold, ill.   II. Title.
PZ8.3.A233 BI 2002   00-044864
[E]—dc21

Typography by Matt Adamec
❖
11 12 13 SCP 20 19 18 17 16 15 14 13 12

black　is brown　is tan

is　　girl　is boy

is　　nose　is

　　　　face

is　　all

　　the

colors

of　　the　　race

is dark   is light
singing   songs
in
singing   night

kiss big woman   hug big man
black   is   brown   is   tan

this is the way it is for us   this is the way we are

i am mom   am mommy   mama mamu   meeny muh
                              and   mom   again
with mighty hugs   and hairbrush mornings
                            catching   curls
later we sit by the window
and   your   head is up against   my chest
we read   and tickle   and   sing the words
                       into the   a i r

go out   to cut wood   for the fire
or cook the corn and chicken legs

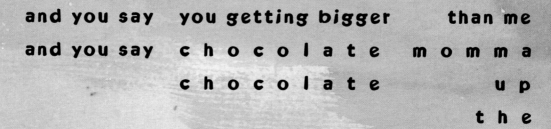

and you say   you getting bigger   than me
and you say   c h o c o l a t e   m o m m a
                c h o c o l a t e   u p
                                                 t h e
                                             m i l k

and *i* say drink the milk
and l a u g h out loud

i am black i am brown   the milk is chocolate brown
i am the c o l o r   of the milk   chocolate cheeks
                            and h a n d s that   darken
                            in   the   s u m m e r   sun

                            a nose that peels brown skin
                                                      in
                                            a u g u s t

i am black   i   am   a   brown   sugar   gown
a   tasty   tan   and   coffee   pumpkin   pie
with   dark brown   eyes   and   almond   ears
and   my   f a c e   gets   ginger   red
when i   puff   and   yell   you   into bed

this is the way it is for us   this is the way we are

i am dad   am daddy   dingbat da
           and   k i s s   me   pa
with the   big   belly   and   the
                         loud   voice
           s i t t i n g   at   my desk
and   you   s i t   on   my   lap
we   read   and   laugh   a n d   pinch
                         t h e   words
           into   t h e   a i r

go out   to cut wood   for the fire
or cook the   corn   and hamburgers

and you say   you getting bigger than me
when i say   d r i n k   t h e m i l k

i am white   the milk   is white
i am not the color of   the milk
i am white   the snow   is white
i am not the color of   the snow

i am white i am white
i am light
with pinks   and   tiny tans
dark hair g r o w i n g on my arms
that d a r k e n in the summer sun

brown eyes
big yellow ears

and my f a c e gets tomato red
when i puff and yell you into bed

this *is* the way *it is* for us   this is the way we are

daddy's sister florence   with the gold gold hair
and momma's tan man   brother
who p l a y s the   frying   p a n

there is granny white   and grandma black
kissing both your cheeks
                           and hugging   back

sitting by the window   telling stories of ago

and you say you getting bigger than all of them

and   pour   a   glass of milk for e v e r y   one

black　　is brown　　is tan
　　is　　girl　　is boy
　　is　　nose　　is
　　　　　　　　　face
　　is　　all
　　　　the
　　colors
of　　the　　race

is dark   is light
singing   songs
in
singing   night

kiss big woman   hug big man
black   is   brown   is   tan

Afterword

When Arnold Adoff and Virginia Hamilton were married in 1960, their marriage violated segregation laws in twenty-eight states in America. Today the U.S. government recognizes sixty-three racial combinations. The 2000 census allowed people to check more than one category under race and ethnic group for the first time. Nearly seven million people—2.4% of the U.S. population—identified their multicultural status.

The Adoffs' two adult children grew up in a progressive Ohio college town among children of many cultural and racial groups. The new version of *black is brown is tan* is an enduring song to them. Generations of young readers and the ones that preceded them have loved this poem. It is a tribute to the diversity of the American family.

We invite readers of all ages to stay strong, and sing along.